The Secret in the Farmhouse

Early Blackbirds 2019

ISBN 978 9001 89133 6

Paula Smith

The Secret in the Farmhouse

2019
Noordhoff Uitgevers BV, Groningen

Any comments concerning this or other publications should be addressed to Noordhoff Uitgevers bv, Afdeling Voortgezet onderwijs, Antwoordnummer 13, 9700 VB Groningen or via the contact form at www.mijnnoordhoff.nl.

FSC www.fsc.org
MIX
Papier van verantwoorde herkomst
FSC® C118189

Illustrations by Elizabeth Botté

ISBN 978 9001 89136 7

Contents

Chapter 1 A beautiful place to stay

'Hey, Dan, watch out! Alex has got her camera out again!' laughed Matt.

'Oh, Alex, how many photographs of us do you need?' asked Dan.

'My phone can take photos too, you know,' teased Matt. He held up his phone to take some photos. 'I'm going to take a photo of this bag ... oh, and the seat, Matt's nose, my knee and you, Alex. Come on, smile for the camera. You can do it. Nice smile for the camera, Alex!'

Alex poked her tongue out at Matt. She didn't mind him teasing her. He was a good friend.

'Ha! A camera takes much better photos than a phone,' said Alex. 'One day I'll be a famous photographer. Everyone will want a photograph by Alex Collins hanging on their wall. You'll see.' She poked her tongue out at Matt again and they both laughed.

'Well, today we just want to be left alone. We do not want to have a camera shoved in our faces all the time,' said Dan moodily.

'Don't be mean, Dan. Alex doesn't "shove" her camera in our faces all the time. She just loves to take photographs. It makes her happy and she's very good at it,' said Hannah, smiling at her friend.

Dan glared at Hannah, but he didn't say anything more.

'How long is this bus ride anyway?' asked Matt.

'Not much longer,' said Alex, trying to lift the mood. 'I'm really looking forward to this week. I looked at Mayfield House on the Internet. It looks like a beautiful place to stay.'

It was Monday morning, and the four friends were on a bus full of students. Each year their school organised a five day trip to a stately home called Mayfield House. This year it was their turn, and they were looking forward to it. Mayfield House was one of the most famous stately homes in England. Now it was a museum full of historical treasures, with a lodge and study centre for school groups.

'The house was built in the 17th century. It belonged to the Langford family. Some cool things happened there over the years,' said Alex.

'What kind of cool things?' asked Hannah.

'Well, there was a fire which destroyed part of the house in 1790. In 1865 Lord Langford's wife fell down the stairs and died. It's believed she was pushed by her husband. Then from 1943 to 1945 the house was used as a hospital to treat wounded soldiers from the Second World War,' said Alex. She loved history and had enjoyed learning about the house.

'So, are you saying there was a murder in the house?' asked Hannah.

'That's what they say. They also say that the house is still haunted by Lady Mary. Some people have said they felt like someone was touching their cheek and neck in the night. It only happened to men and they always looked a little bit like Lord Langford!' said Alex.

'Oh, that's scary. I hope neither of you two looks like him.' Hannah looked at Matt and Dan.

'I think we'll be safe,' laughed Matt. 'We're not staying in the main house anyway, remember.'

'Why not?' said Hannah.

'They can't let a group of school students stay in a nice house like that,' said Dan.

From the seat in front of them, Ethan said, 'Yeah, someone might steal some of the historical treasures!' He turned round and looked over the seat at Dan.

'Shut up, Ethan,' said Matt. He looked at his friend. Dan was standing up, and his face was red with anger. He glared at Ethan.

Ethan laughed nastily. 'What is it, Dan? Do you have something to say?'

'I think you should do like Matt suggested and shut up!' said Dan.

'Or what? Are you going to make me? Or maybe you just need a tissue so you can have a little cry?' laughed Ethan.

Dan started to reach over the seat, 'Why, you –'

'Dan, don't listen to him,' Matt said quickly. 'Forget about it. Sit down.'

Matt put his hand on Dan's arm. Dan tried to shake it off, but Matt squeezed his arm.

'Dan, he's not worth it! Come on, sit down.' He gave Dan's arm another squeeze and said again, 'He's not worth it!'

Finally he felt Dan relax, and they both sat down. Dan stared out of the window. His face was still red, his eyes hard with anger.

Twenty minutes later the bus drove into the grounds of Mayfield House. They drove up a long driveway. The house was surrounded by beautiful gardens and woods. There was a stone wall that separated the house and gardens from the fields beyond.

Hannah, Alex, Matt and Dan climbed down the steps of the bus. They looked up at the house. It was a very large, beautiful stone building. Some old worn steps led up to a big wooden door. There were lines of windows on each side of the doors. There were more windows on the first and second floor, and even some smaller ones in the roof.

'Wow! What a beautiful place. It's much nicer in real life,' said Alex. 'I can't wait to –'

'– take some photos!' shouted her three friends together.

'Oh, you guys,' said Alex.

They all laughed and picked up their bags. They joined the rest of the students standing in front of the house.

One of the teachers, Mr Jones, stood on the steps of the house with a lady beside him. He called out, 'Attention, everyone. Listen, please! I know you've been sitting on the bus for a while. You will have plenty of time explore, but first I would

like to introduce Miss Holt. She's the director of Mayfield House and is here to welcome us.'

Miss Holt smiled and said, 'Good morning. Welcome to Mayfield House. This wonderful old house has stood here for nearly 300 years. You will be learning a lot about its history over the next few days. Sadly we can no longer allow people to stay in the house. As you can imagine, there are a lot of valuable historical treasures to protect. We also have to care for the building itself. After 300 years some of the floors are quite worn and need to be looked after. We must ask that you do not enter the house without a teacher. You will have a tour of it later in the week. Now, I'd like to introduce you to Mr Baker and Miss Patel. They are two of our amazing Education Officers who will be looking after you this week. In a moment, they will take you over to the lodge, where you are going to stay. You have everything you need there. Once you have unpacked, there will be a lovely lunch ready for you. I'm happy to tell you that we have a great chef and the food is delicious. I hope you all have a wonderful stay with us.'

'Thank you,' said Mrs Turner, another of their teachers. 'I am sure we'll have a great week.'

The students chatted excitedly as they followed the Education Officers down a path to the lodge. It was a modern building, but it had been built to look like a smaller model of the main house. It was hidden from the house by trees and had a beautiful garden around it.

'Oh, this is lovely,' said Hannah as they walked up to the front door. 'I didn't think it would be this nice. I love the gardens.'

'I wonder if the food is as good as she said,' said Matt.

'Delicious, she said! Food before comfort for you, isn't it Matt? I want to know what the beds are like,' said Alex.

'I bet it'll be bunk beds,' said Dan.

'Oh, no! I hate bunk beds. I want a four-poster bed,' said Alex. 'I'd love to sleep in a four-poster bed!'

The friends laughed as they followed the others into the house.

Two hours later the students had unpacked and eaten lunch. They were waiting for their teachers in the dining room of the lodge.

'Okay, everyone. I hope you have all unpacked and settled in. I know you are all ready to work hard this week,' said Mrs Turner. 'You've all got your history projects to work on.'

A few students groaned and everyone laughed.

'Don't worry,' she added. 'We're going to have lots of fun too.'

Then Mr Jones stood next to her. He said, 'We've organised lots of good activities for you. Tomorrow you'll be doing an orienteering activity. You'll be in small groups and you'll use maps to find your way across the countryside. It will be a race to see who can get back to the house first.'

There were some more groans from the students.

'A day of fresh air and exercise will be good for you,' said Mr Jones cheerfully.

'Why do adults love fresh air and exercise so much?' Matt said quietly to Hannah.

'Oh, it will be fun,' said Hannah. 'At least it's better than sitting in a classroom. And maybe we can win.'

'You always want to win,' said Dan meanly. Hannah opened her mouth to say something, but then changed her mind. Dan was in a permanently bad mood at the moment. It was probably best not to argue with him.

Mr Jones continued, 'This afternoon you'll work in your groups. You'll do some map-reading practice. We're going to start work in the classroom. Then you'll have some time to practice what you've learnt in the grounds. We'll finish at four o'clock. You will have some free time before supper. But please remember you cannot go in Mayfield House. So when I call out your name, please go to the classroom and wait in your groups.'

Mr Jones began calling out students' names. The four friends waited for him to call theirs. But he didn't, and he left the room with the other students. The friends looked at each other.

'What's going on?' whispered Alex.

'I don't know,' said Hannah looking puzzled.

'I think I do,' said Dan, looking angry.

Mrs Turner came over to them.

'I need to talk to Dan,' she said. 'But you four are working as a team, so I want you all to hear this. Perhaps you know, Dan, that some teachers are unhappy with your attitude at the moment. They did not want you to come this week.'

'But that's –' Dan started angrily.

Mrs Turner held up her hand. 'Dan, please let me finish. I am not one of those teachers. I believe that you can be a good student, if you can control your temper. I know it has been a difficult year for you. Mr Jones told me that things at home have been a little complicated.'

Dan looked at the ground. His cheeks were red. He hated the teachers talking about him. Mrs Turner was right, things were complicated. His dad had left them six months ago. There had been no warning, although he had to admit his parents had been arguing a lot. His dad had never said a word to him or his sister. He just left one day. Dan had come home from school to find his mum crying. After that things got really bad. His mum cried a lot. Then there was the money – or lack of it. His mum had taken a second job to try and pay the bills. His mum and dad were still arguing all the time, mostly over money, and about him and his sister. He was supposed to see his dad but he refused to. He was too angry with him. He hated to see his mum and sister so sad. He hated his dad for leaving.

Dan looked up. He realized Mrs Turner was still talking to him.

'But it was wrong to have those fights with Ethan and Chris. And it was very wrong to steal things from that shop. Now that you are in trouble with the police, you have to be very careful, Dan. The head teacher has told me that you have no more chances. If you get into any trouble this week, we will have to send you home. The head teacher will want to speak to you. He will probably expel you from our school. Do you understand?'

Dan nodded his head and said, 'Yes, Mrs Turner.'

Then Mrs Turner said to the others, 'I hope you three are going to help Dan this week. He does need to control his temper.' Hannah, Alex and Matt nodded too.

As they turned to leave, Mrs Turner said 'And Dan, try to stay away from Ethan and Chris. I don't want to see you boys fighting again. I do know what Ethan can be like. Please try and avoid him. I really don't want to see you expelled from our school. Okay?'

Hannah stepped forward and said, 'It's okay, Mrs Turner. We'll help Dan. There won't be any more trouble.'

Mrs Turner smiled, 'Thank you, Hannah. Dan is very lucky to have friends like you that he can depend on.'

Mrs Turner walked away, and Dan turned to Hannah.

'Why did you say that?' he said to her.

'Say what?' asked Hannah.

'That you're going to help me stay out of trouble! I'm not some little kid that you have to look after, you know!' he said angrily.

Hannah took a step back, surprised by his anger, 'I know, I don't think that. I just wanted Mrs Turner to leave you alone. I –'

'Well, I don't need you to help me. Stay out of my business. *Got it?*' Dan turned and marched out of the room.

'Oh, dear,' said Alex.

Hannah turned to Alex and Matt. She looked upset. 'I didn't mean to make him angry,' she said. Her voice was shaking.

'We know that,' said Matt, putting an arm around her shoulders. 'You know what he's like at the moment.'

'But I don't understand why he is so angry with *me* all the time,' replied Hannah.

'I think he's just angry with life right now,' said Alex. 'Come on, let's go and find him. We need to start the map work.'

'Hopefully he's calmed down a bit,' said Matt. 'It will be okay, Hannah. Come on, cheer up.'

Chapter 2 The old farmhouse

On Tuesday morning the students stood outside in their groups chatting. They were looking forward to a day away from books and teachers.

'Good morning, everyone, if I can have your attention please?' Mr Jones called out to them. 'I hope you are ready for a fun day in the countryside. Have you all got your backpacks?' The students all nodded. 'Each group must have their lunch, water, a map and a mobile phone. I've got your maps here.'

He gave the maps out, one for each group, then he continued, 'Do you see the six red triangles on the map? You have to find your way to those six places. When you arrive at each place, you need to find the answer to a question. The six questions are on the back of your maps. The number next to the question matches the number in the red triangle.'

The students turned their maps over to look, and everyone started talking.

Mr Jones held up his hand for quiet. 'Don't try to answer the questions now,' he said. 'You can only find the answers at those six places. The first group to come back with all six answers will be the winners. It doesn't matter which way you go. You can decide which triangle to go to first. Please be careful out there. We trust you all to behave yourselves, so please do not let us down. You all have my mobile phone number, so you can call me if you need to. And remember – have fun! All right, let's begin.'

The groups all started talking at once about the best way to go. Some of the groups started to walk down the drive to the front gates.

Matt held the map. Hannah pointed at a red triangle with a number two on it. 'Let's go to this red triangle first,' she said. 'We can go across these fields.'

'Can't we walk along the roads? I don't want to walk through muddy fields,' said Alex.

'We have to go the quickest way,' said Dan. 'Don't forget, it's a race.'

'And we don't want to just follow all the other groups,' said Matt.

They watched some of the others. The groups were turning left when they got to the road.

'Okay, we can turn right and follow the road to here,' said Dan. He pointed at the map. 'Then we can take the footpath across the fields until we get to Hannah's red triangle.'

'Okay,' said Alex. She had her camera out and was taking photos of her friends.

After about ten minutes walking along the road, they came to the footpath through the fields. They followed the footpath for about fifteen minutes until Matt said, 'Okay, we're at the red triangle on the map.'

'So, what are we looking for?' said Dan, looking around. There wasn't much to see. They were standing where two narrow lanes crossed. Apart from trees, hedges and fields, there was nothing around them.

'What's the question we have to answer?' asked Hannah.

Matt looked for question two on the back of the map. He read out the question. 'How many miles to the village of Thornley?'

'How are we supposed to find that out?' asked Dan.

'There!' said Hannah. 'There's a sign by the path up there.'

They ran to the sign and Alex read, 'Thornley 9 Miles.'

'Easy!' said Matt, and he wrote the answer on the map.

'This is fun,' said Alex. 'Do you think the other groups have got to a triangle yet?'

'I don't know, but let's keep moving,' said Hannah. She pointed at the map. 'Let's go to this triangle next, number four. That's the closest. We can follow this footpath and get there in half the time. I bet everyone else is just using the roads.'

The group agreed, and they continued along another footpath.

Alex stopped suddenly. 'I just felt some rain,' she said.

'I didn't feel anything,' said Hannah. 'Oh, wait, you're right. I just felt a few drops too.'

Alex stopped and took off her backpack. She reached inside for her raincoat.

'You don't need a raincoat, Alex,' said Matt. 'It's only a little bit of rain. I'm sure it will stop soon.'

But he was wrong. The rain didn't stop. Twenty minutes later they heard thunder too.

'Look at those black clouds,' said Dan. As they looked at the sky, the rain started to pour down.

'Quick, let's get under that tree,' shouted Hannah.

'This isn't fun anymore,' said Alex. 'I hate rain, and I hate storms even more!'

There was a flash of lightning, and more thunder.

'That's really close,' said Hannah. 'I don't think we should stay under this tree.'

'What? You want to walk in that rain and get soaking wet?' asked Matt.

'No, but I don't want to stay under a tree that might get hit by lightning and fall on me,' answered Hannah.

'Look. There's a farmhouse down there,' said Dan. He pointed down into a valley. There was a farmhouse and a big barn with a stone wall and trees around it. 'I'm sure the farmer will let us shelter from the rain.'

'That sounds good. Let's go!' said Alex.

They ran down the footpath towards the farm. Dan was the first to arrive at the farmhouse. 'Hey! There's no one here,' he shouted to the others. 'The place is empty. All the windows are broken!'

'Try the door,' said Hannah. 'Does it open?'

Dan opened the door. The four friends walked into the farmhouse.

Matt called out, 'Hello?' There was no answer.

They looked around the room. The wooden floor was worn and dusty. There was a large old fireplace and small windows with old, torn curtains. The walls were covered with torn, faded wallpaper. The only furniture in the room was four old chairs and a small table.

The friends took off their wet raincoats and hung them over the back of the chairs.

'This place is wonderful,' cried Alex. 'Look at this beautiful old fireplace!' She took her camera out of her bag and took a few photos.

'What do you think happened to the people who lived here?' asked Hannah.

'I don't know,' said Alex. 'It looks like it's been empty for a long time.'

'I'm hungry,' said Dan. 'Why don't we have lunch here?'

'We might as well,' said Matt. 'It's raining even harder now.'

They got their lunches out of their backpacks. Matt used a tissue to wipe dust off the chairs. They made themselves comfortable.

'I hope the storm doesn't last long,' said Hannah. 'We won't have time to get to any more of the red triangles.'

'I know, I didn't expect to enjoy this activity at all,' said Alex. 'But it's actually really good fun.'

'I'm sure the storm will pass soon. I don't mind walking in the rain if it isn't too heavy,' said Hannah.

The others laughed.

'You really want to win, don't you?' said Matt.

'There's nothing wrong with liking to win,' said Hannah crossly. She looked at her friends smiling at her and laughed. 'Yes I know, I can be a little competitive.'

They chatted together as they ate their lunches. The thunder was moving further away, but it was still raining hard. Matt got the map out of his bag and they looked at the red triangles.

'I think we should follow the road now,' he said. 'The footpaths will be muddy after all this rain.'

The others all agreed. They studied the map and planned the best way to go. They wanted to find all the answers to the rest of the questions.

'Well we can't go anywhere yet,' said Alex looking out the window. 'I want to look around and take some more photos.' She picked up her camera and left the room.

A few minutes later Alex called out from one of the other rooms, 'Hey, guys! Look in here. There are lots of boxes. They don't look very old.'

The other three found Alex in a small room at the back of the house. They looked at the boxes. There were a lot of them, some piled on top of others.

Hannah opened a box and looked inside.

'Wow! It's full of nice things,' she said. She pulled out a large silver bowl and a silver candlestick.

Matt opened another box and said, 'Hey, look at this. There are some mobile phones, and a laptop too. Why are all these things here?'

'I don't know,' said Hannah. 'There's jewellery in this one.' She held up a necklace. 'Do you think these are real diamonds?'

'Hey, look at this,' said Dan. He pulled a knife out of a box.

'Wow! That's not an old knife. It looks very new. It looks like it is meant for hurting people,' said Matt.

'Oh, I don't like this. Please put it back,' cried Alex.

'Yes, I agree with Alex,' said Hannah. 'This doesn't feel right. Let's put it all back – just the way we found it.'

'Yes good idea,' said Dan. They put the things back and closed the boxes. Matt moved them back to where they had found them.

He looked out of the window and said, 'Look it's stopped raining. We can go.'

They walked back to the front room. They moved the chairs back and picked up their empty lunch bags. They picked up their raincoats and backpacks and walked to the front door.

Suddenly, Dan said, 'Look!' and pointed out of a window beside the front door.

A white van was pulling up outside.

'Quick, let's go out the back,' said Matt.

The friends turned and ran down the hall. Dan opened the back door and ran out. Hannah followed close behind.

Then Alex stopped just as she got to the door and said, 'Oh, no! I've left my camera in the room with the boxes!'

Matt said, 'Alex, there isn't time –' But Alex had already gone back to pick up her camera.

'Got it!' she said. As she came out of the room, the front door started to open.

'Quick,' Matt whispered. 'They'll see us. Hide in here.'

Matt opened the door nearest to him. It was an old bathroom. Alex and Matt went inside and shut the door quickly. They heard people coming into the house.

'How are we going to get out?' Alex whispered.

'I don't know. We'll just have to wait,' replied Matt.

They could hear three men talking and coming down the hall. The men went into the small room with the boxes.

Matt quietly opened the bathroom door. He and Alex listened. They heard a man say, 'We'll just take these three boxes today. George doesn't want too many boxes at one time. He said it makes it hard to get rid of the stuff.'

'But it's not safe to leave them here. I don't want to keep driving all the way out here to pick up a couple of boxes. Can't we just fill the van and leave them in there for a couple of days?' said the second man.

'Don't be stupid!' said the first man. 'Where do we put them? They're safer here than in the van. What if it gets stolen? Nobody comes to this old place. It's been empty for years.'

Then the third man said, 'Well, I need to go to the bathroom first.'

Matt and Alex looked at each other, their eyes wide with fear.

The first man said, 'Hey come back here. Help move the boxes first. Then you can go to the bathroom. I don't want to be hanging around waiting for you.'

Matt and Alex heard the men lift the boxes. Matt quickly closed the bathroom door as the men came out of the room carrying a box each.

Matt felt scared. He looked at Alex. She looked like she was going to cry. Matt put his fingers to his lips. He opened the door again and peered through a crack. The men were walking out to the van. They had their backs to them. Then he pointed to the door and pulled Alex's arm gently.

'Quickly,' he whispered. 'Out the back door before they come back in.'

They ran out the room and straight to the back door. Matt opened it quickly and they went out as quietly as they could.

They saw Dan and Hannah hiding in the doorway of the old barn. They ran over to join them.

'That was close,' said Matt, taking a deep breath.

'Alex, are you okay?' asked Dan. Alex looked white as a sheet.

'I was so scared. I thought that guy was going to come in and find us,' said Alex. 'Do you think they'll come in here?'

'No, I don't think so,' said Dan. 'There's nothing here except that old tractor.'

'But we should get away from this place,' said Hannah. 'We've checked the map. There's the road out of here or the footpath back across the fields.'

'No, not the road,' said Matt. 'That's the way they came in. Let's go back across the fields. I know it will be muddy, but I don't want them to see us near the farmhouse.'

'What about the orienteering?' asked Alex.

'Forget about the orienteering!' said Hannah. 'I think we should get back to Mayfield House as quickly as possible.'

They ran around the back of the barn, through some trees and back to the footpath. Nobody spoke until they were well away from the farm.

Hannah was the first to break the silence. 'How many boxes were there, do you think?'

'Twenty, maybe,' replied Matt.

'More. Maybe thirty,' said Dan.

'I think those three men are robbers,' said Hannah. 'I think they've stolen all those things in the boxes.'

'Yes, I think you're right,' said Alex. 'Do you think we should tell someone? A teacher? Or maybe we should go to the police?'

'Why do we have to tell anyone?' asked Dan. 'We don't know that they are robbers. You heard what Mrs Turner said. Any trouble and they'll send me home.'

'I agree with Dan,' said Matt. 'We don't need to tell anyone.'

'What do you think, Hannah?' asked Alex.

'Well, it's true,' replied Hannah. 'We don't really know anything about it. I mean it is suspicious but we don't have any real proof. I don't think we need to tell anyone. They would probably think we are making it up anyway.'

They had reached the road back to Mayfield House. As they turned onto the road, a white van drove past. The man beside the window stared at them.

'Oh, that's them, isn't it?' said Alex. 'They scare me.'

Matt looked at the number plate on the back of the van. 'JQ54PS' he said and wrote it down on the back of the map.

'Let's get back, I've had enough excitement for one day,' said Hannah. 'I hope we aren't the only group that didn't finish the race.'

'No, I'm sure the others all came back as soon as it started to rain,' said Matt. 'Come on. Hannah's right, let's get back. I'm hungry and someone told me the afternoon cakes are ...'

'... delicious?' said Alex. 'Last one back gets the smallest piece.' She ran down the road and others chased after her laughing.

Chapter 3 A tour of Mayfield House

On Wednesday morning all the students walked over to Mayfield House. Today was the day they were going to have their tour.

'I can't wait to see inside,' said Alex.

'Yes, I want to see how the people used to live here,' said Hannah.

They walked over to the front of the house. Miss Holt was waiting on the steps.

'Welcome everyone. I hope you are all enjoying your stay,' she said. 'Now, for this morning's tour, you will be in three groups. Our guides will show you round. Please listen carefully to your guide. I know you will find the tour very interesting.'

A friendly woman came over and said, 'All right. You students over here, you'll be in my group. Follow me please.'

'Oh, no,' said Alex quietly. 'Ethan and Chris are in our group.'

The woman walked around to the back of the house and the students followed her. Mrs Turner joined the group. The guide stopped in front of a small doorway and turned to face them all.

'Well, hello everyone. My name is Sarah, and I'm your guide for the tour. We are going to start here in the kitchens of the old house. I have to admit it's one of my favourite parts of the house. You will see where the servants worked. A place this size had over thirty staff to run the house and gardens. Later I'll show you where they slept up there.' Sarah pointed to the small windows in the roof of the house.

Alex took lots of photos as the group moved from room to room. Sarah told them all about the jobs that the servants did. She took them into the large kitchen and showed them the type of food they ate. Finally she stopped in front of an old staircase.

'We are going to go upstairs now. I'm going to show you how the Lord and Lady of the house lived. We have arranged the house to show you what it looked like in the 1700s, 1800s and 1900s. We even have a room set up just like it was in the Second World War, when the house was used as a hospital. Follow me please.'

Upstairs the house was very different. The rooms were large and filled with old historical treasures. As they moved from room to room Dan noticed something strange.

'Hey, have you noticed that guy over there?' said Dan.

'What? The security guard?' asked Matt.

'Yeah. He's followed us into every room,' said Dan. 'Don't those guys usually just stay in one room? It feels like he's watching us.'

'I know why!' said Ethan. He looked at Dan with a nasty smile.

Dan raised his fist and said, 'I'm going to –'

But Matt put his hand on Dan's arm and said, 'Don't, Dan.'

Dan looked at his friend, took a deep breath and lowered his fist.

Ethan laughed nastily as he moved away.

'Don't take any notice of Ethan and Chris,' Matt said. 'Don't forget it wasn't just you who got into trouble after that fight. They got into trouble too. Ethan's still angry with you. He is just trying to make you fight him. He wants you to be expelled from the school.'

'Yeah, I know,' said Dan.

The boys turned and saw Mrs Turner. She was watching them from the other side of the room.

'It feels like the whole world is watching me,' said Dan angrily.

'Mrs Turner is on your side, remember that,' said Matt.

As they walked through the house, Sarah pointed out some of the most important objects in the rooms.

'Oh, look,' cried Alex. She pointed to a large four poster bed in one of the bedrooms.

'Oh, I'd love to jump on that bed.'

Sarah laughed, 'I don't think you'd like it very much. The mattress is made of straw. It is very uncomfortable.'

'Oh,' said Alex, looking disappointed.

Finally they made their way to the Great Hall. There was one question Alex had to ask.

'Is it true what they say? Is there a ghost in the house?' she asked.

'Ah, you mean Lady Mary,' said Sarah. 'No one knows what happened the night she fell down the stairs. Some people believed it was Lord Langford. Others believed they were very happy together and it was just a terrible accident. But yes, there have been many people over the years who say they have seen Lady Mary. Or should I say, 'felt' Lady Mary – no one actually sees her. They just feel a very light touch. It's always on the cheek and throat. It only ever happens to men.'

'Men who look a bit like Lord Langford,' said Alex.

'Yes, that's right. Here, I'll show you.' She led them to the staircase. There were large paintings of people all over the walls. She pointed to a painting of a pretty young woman.

'There. That's Lady Mary,' she said. 'And that's Lord Langford beside her.'

'Hey, Ethan,' one of the boys called out. 'He looks a bit like you, don't you think?'

'Yeah, you're right, Simon,' agreed another boy. 'Better be careful, Ethan. Lady Mary might visit you in the night!'

The students all laughed. Ethan glared at them but said nothing.

The tour was over. Sarah led the students out of the house.

Matt looked behind them. The security guard was watching the students leave.

'Rover's still following us,' Matt said to the others.

'Rover? Why Rover?' asked Alex.

'He's like a dog that won't leave you alone!' laughed Matt.

They watched the security guard go back into Mayfield House.

Then Hannah said, 'Hey, look, there's a police car.'

The police car was parked in front of the house. Two police officers were talking to Miss Holt.

'What do they want?' asked Alex.

Sarah was near, and she heard Alex's question. 'Sadly, we had a robbery here last week,' she said. 'The police are here to ask some more questions.'

'A robbery?' said Hannah.

'Yes. They took things from the office: laptops, mobile phones, that kind of thing,' said Sarah. 'And some silver things from some of the rooms too – candlesticks, bowls and things. Even some jewellery. It's terrible. I really hope we can get the things back.' Then she turned and spoke to all the students.

'Thank you all for listening. I've enjoyed showing you around our beautiful house. I hope you have enjoyed it too.'

The students all thanked Sarah. Hannah waited for her to walk away, and then she said to her friends, 'Did you hear that? That's what we saw yesterday at the farmhouse.'

'Yes,' said Alex. 'I think they stole it from here. What do you think we should do?'

'I think we should talk to the police,' said Hannah.

'Hannah, we don't have any proof,' said Matt. 'We know there was a robbery here. And we know what we saw in that farmhouse. But we don't know enough to put the two things together.'

'Alex,' said Hannah. 'Did you take any photos of the things in that room yesterday?'

'No,' replied Alex. 'I was just so surprised to see it all. I'm so silly. Sorry.'

'That's okay,' said Hannah. 'But we have to say something.'

'What do you think, Dan?' asked Alex.

Dan was quiet for a moment. Then he said, 'I suppose Hannah's right. It has to be the stuff we saw yesterday. We should tell the police, but I don't want to talk to them. Please don't ask me to talk to them.'

'No, okay,' said Hannah. 'I can talk to them. Alex, will you come with me?'

'Yes, sure, if you think they'll listen to us,' she said.

Dan and Matt watched the girls go and talk to the police and Miss Holt. They saw Hannah point to them. One of the policemen wrote something in a small notebook.

'Oh, no,' said Dan. 'I hope they don't call us over.'

But they didn't. Hannah and Alex came back.

'What did they say?' asked Matt.

'Not much, really,' said Alex. 'They took some notes about the farmhouse and the van, and they took our names. That was all. They're going to go and have a look.'

'You didn't give them my name, did you?' asked Dan.

'Well, we had to, Dan. Don't be silly,' said Hannah angrily. 'You're not England's most wanted robber, you know.'

'I know that, thanks,' said Dan. He walked off.

'That was unkind, Hannah,' said Alex. 'You know how hard he's trying.'

'Okay, okay, I know,' said Hannah.

In the lodge later that day, Mrs Turner came into the dining room. 'I need Dan, Matt, Alex and Hannah in the study room, please,' she said.

The four students followed Mrs Turner into the study room. The two police officers who the girls had talked to were there.

'This is Officer Bryant and Officer Howes. They tell me that you girls talked with them this morning,' said Mrs Turner.

'Hello again,' said Officer Bryant. 'I've talked to Mrs Turner, but I wanted to talk to you too. We went to the farmhouse after we spoke to you, but we found nothing there.'

'What? Nothing?' said Matt.

'But there were boxes,' said Hannah. 'We all saw them. Are you sure you looked properly?'

'Hannah, I think the officers know how to do their job, don't you?' said Mrs Turner.

'I don't know what you saw,' said Officer Howes. 'We looked in every room and there were no boxes there at all. But we thank you for telling us about it. It's always better to tell the police if you think you see something strange.'

The police officers turned their attention to Dan.

'Dan, we understand that you have been in a bit of trouble with the police,' said Officer Bryant. 'Mrs Turner tells us that you need to be very careful.'

Dan's face turned red. He looked down at the ground.

'It might be a good idea if you just do your schoolwork,' said Officer Howes. 'Stay away from old farmhouses.'

'Yes, I quite agree,' said Mrs Turner.

The officers and Mrs Turner left the room.

'Are you happy now?' Dan asked Hannah angrily. He marched out of the room.

Hannah sighed. 'I'm not sure it was a good idea to talk to the police. Now Mrs Turner is cross with us too. We've just made everything worse,' she said sadly.

Chapter 4 In town

On Thursday morning at breakfast, the friends were still talking about the farmhouse. All except for Dan. He sat quietly, deep in his own thoughts.

'I don't understand why the police didn't find anything at the house,' said Matt. 'We all saw it there, didn't we?'

'I know, it's really strange,' said Hannah. 'I keep playing it over and over in my mind. Those boxes were definitely there. And I'm sure we saw some of the things stolen from the house.'

'I didn't like the way those police officers talked to us last night,' said Matt. 'I don't think they believed us. They think we're making it all up.'

'That's exactly what they think,' said Hannah. 'Silly school kids making things up.'

'Can we just forget about it, please?' begged Alex. 'We did the right thing. We told the police. That's all we needed to do. There's probably a really good explanation. Come on, we're going to the cathedral today. It is going to be really interesting. And we've got some free time in town this afternoon. I want to forget about the farmhouse and the boxes. I just want to go shopping and have some fun.'

Hannah smiled at her friend. 'Alex is right. There's nothing more we can do anyway. Let's have fun today. Forget about the farmhouse and the boxes.'

'I agree,' said Matt. 'Dan?'

'What?' said Dan. He looked at them as though he'd forgotten they were there.

'What's up with you?' asked Matt. 'You're a million miles away today. We were just saying we're going to forget about what we saw at the farmhouse. We're going to enjoy the trip into town today and have some fun.'

'Yeah, sure. Suits me.' replied Dan.

Hannah looked at Dan for a moment. She knew she needed to say something to him.

'Dan, I'm sorry I said those things yesterday,' she said awkwardly. 'I know things have been difficult for you at home. And I know how hard you're trying.'

'Forget it,' said Dan grumpily.

'Why are you so angry with me?' asked Hannah.

'Hannah, you heard Dan, just forget it,' said Matt.

'No, I won't forget it,' replied Hannah. She was getting angry herself now. 'You've been snapping at me for weeks now. Even when I'm trying to be your friend, you treat me like your enemy. You don't do it to the others. You don't snap at them all the time. I want to know why!'

Dan looked at her for a minute. Then he shook his head in amazement.

'Are you kidding me!' he said. 'You have no idea why I might be angry?'

'Well, I know you're upset with everything that's going on at home,' Hannah replied, 'But I don't see why that makes you angry at me.'

'I don't believe you don't know,' he said. 'You told them I was in the shop!'

'Told who? What shop?' Hannah was confused. 'I don't know what you're talking about.'

'You told the police you saw me in the shop,' he said. 'When they said I stole that stuff.'

'I didn't speak to the police!' cried Hannah.

'But they said there were witnesses, and apart from my little sister Natalie and I there was only you and the shopkeeper in the shop,' said Dan.

'Well, I didn't say anything, because I didn't speak to the police,' said Hannah. 'It must have been someone else. I didn't see you steal anything. I wasn't even near you in the shop. I can't believe you think I'd tell the police that.' Hannah was shocked and upset. 'I don't understand why you did it anyway,' she continued, holding back her tears. 'What was the point of stealing a couple of bars of chocolate?'

Dan looked down at the floor. 'Don't know, just felt like it, I suppose,' he muttered.

'But you were with Natalie,' said Hannah. 'It's not a very good example to set your sister, is it?'

'Hannah ...' warned Matt, watching his friend closely.

Dan said nothing, but his face turned a deep red.

Alex had been listening and she suddenly realised something. 'Hang on,' she said slowly. 'I don't believe you stole anything at all. It was Natalie wasn't it? She stole the chocolate. Of course, that makes so much more sense.'

Matt and Hannah both stared at Dan.

'Is it true, Dan?' asked Matt, quietly. 'Was it Natalie?'

Dan didn't say anything. He just stared at the ground. Then he slowly nodded his head.

'Oh, Dan' cried Alex. 'You were just protecting Natalie. All those horrible things people are saying about you. You did nothing wrong.'

'She didn't mean to do it. She's so angry and confused at the moment,' said Dan. 'I don't think she was really thinking clearly.'

'You're a good brother to take the blame for her,' said Matt, patting his friend on the shoulder.

'I'm not just protecting Natalie – it's my mum too. She would be so upset if she found out about Natalie. She'd blame herself.'

'But she's upset with you too,' said Hannah. 'And you got into trouble with the police.'

'Yeah, I know, but I'm older. It's different, somehow,' said Dan, shrugging. 'Anyway, I don't care about the police. That shopkeeper shouldn't have called them. It was only a couple of bars of chocolate. He just said he was sick of kids stealing from him. He just wanted revenge. He was so mean!'

Dan looked at Hannah, 'You know, I bet he got someone to say they were in the shop. So that he had a witness. I know you wouldn't say anything to the police. I don't know why I thought it was you. Sorry, Hannah.'

'It's okay,' said Hannah, she gave his arm a gentle squeeze. 'I'm glad you told us the truth, Dan.'

Dan smiled shyly at his three friends. He was glad he had told them too. He felt better now they knew. But there was still something that was worrying him.

'You won't tell anyone will you?' he asked.

'No! Of course not,' they replied together.

They were all feeling much more cheerful as they rode in the bus with all the others to the nearby town.

They had a tour of the cathedral first. As usual, Alex took a lot of photos. They also had a worksheet to complete with questions about the cathedral and cemetery outside. As they walked around the cemetery Matt stopped in front of one of the gravestones. He pointed to the old, worn writing on the stone.

'Hey Alex, isn't this your ghost?' he asked.

Alex bent down and read the writing on the gravestone.

In loving memory of
Lady Mary Longford 1843–1865

'Oh, she was so young,' said Alex sadly. 'I'd love to know what happened that night. I believe he did push her down the stairs.'

Hannah came and looked over her shoulder.

'It is sad. I wonder why he did it.'

'You don't really know that he pushed her,' said Dan. 'It's probably just a story they tell. Every old house is expected to have a ghost.'

'Well, I *do* believe it,' said Alex. She took some photos of the gravestone for her project.

The students ate their lunch on the grass in front of the cathedral. When they had finished, Mrs Turner stood up to talk to them all. 'Now, I know everyone wants to do more school work –' The students all laughed. '– but instead, you get some free time.'

There was a loud cheer.

'We are going to walk down the hill into the town centre,' Mrs Turner continued. 'We will meet under the clock in the square at three o'clock. So you have two hours of free time. If anyone has any problems, call us on our mobiles.'

All the students were happy as they walked down the hill.

'Well, what do you guys want to do?' Alex asked her three friends.

'I want to find a computer games shop,' said Dan.

'I want to look in some charity shops. They usually have some good clothes,' said Hannah.

'What's it to be, Matt?' laughed Alex. 'Clothes first, or games?'

'Hmm ... I'm going to have to say games!' replied Matt. 'Why don't Dan and I go to the games shop and you guys go clothes shopping? Then we can meet up in an hour and have a milk-shake or something.'

'That's a good idea. Hannah?' Alex turned to ask her friend beside her. But she was gone. Alex looked around. Hannah was looking down a small side street.

'Hey guys, come here,' she called. They walked over to Hannah and she pointed down the side street. 'Look down there. It's the white van we saw at the farmhouse the other day.'

'Don't all white vans look the same?' asked Dan.

'It's got the same number plate,' said Matt. 'JQ54PS.'

'Well, what it's doing outside that antique shop?' said Hannah. 'Let's go and have a look.'

'I thought we were going to forget about all that,' said Alex.

'We're just looking,' said Matt.

They walked down the street and looked in the window of the antique shop.

'I can't see anyone in there,' said Hannah. 'Let's go in.'

'No!' said Alex. 'We agreed, remember? We're going to forget about all that.'

'Well, let's go around to the back of the shop. Maybe we'll see something,' said Matt.

'Please, let's not get into any trouble,' said Dan. 'I've had enough "little chats" with Mrs Turner.'

'Yes, come on, let's just go shopping,' begged Alex.

'You two stay here. Matt and I will go,' said Hannah. 'We're not going to do anything. We just want to have a quick look.'

Hannah and Matt walked down a narrow lane to the back of the shops. As they reached the back of the antique shop, they could see two men in a window. They were arguing.

Hannah and Matt hid behind a car.

'I wish we were close enough to hear what they are saying,' said Hannah.

Matt looked over the car just as one of the men looked out of the window.

'Hey! No, it can't be,' whispered Matt, bending down out of sight.

'Can't be what?' said Hannah.

'That's the security guard from the house,' Matt said.

'What – Rover?' asked Hannah. 'Are you sure?'

'I think so,' said Matt, but the man had turned away from the window.

'Let's just watch them for a minute. He might turn back around and we can see his face properly,' said Matt.

They waited quietly, watching the men in the window. They were still arguing.

'Hey, Hannah,' said Matt thoughtfully. 'I wanted to talk to you alone. I've been thinking about what Dan told us today.'

'Yeah, me too,' said Hannah. 'I can't believe how much he's been through this year.'

'I know,' said Matt. 'And it makes me really angry that he has to put up with Ethan. He picks on Dan all the time.'

'I've been wondering about something. Why did Ethan try and give Dan a tissue on the bus?' asked Hannah.

'It's because someone was talking about their dad in the changing rooms after sport. Dan started to cry. It was just after his dad had left them.'

'Oh, poor Dan. No wonder he hates Ethan so much. I hate him too, he's such a bully,' said Hannah.

'What if we could teach Ethan a lesson? Maybe get him to leave Dan alone?' asked Matt.

'I'd love that, but how?' asked Hannah.

'I'll tell you later, but we can't tell Dan or Alex. We can't tell anyone.' said Matt. 'If Ethan finds out he'll never leave any of us alone again.'

'Sounds interesting. Okay, I'm happy to do anything to keep Ethan away from Dan,' said Hannah.

'Rover still hasn't turned around!' said Matt. 'I wonder what they are arguing about.'

'Oh, look they're leaving the room,' said Hannah.

'Quick – let's go back around to the front. Maybe we'll see him get into the van.'

But when they got to the front of the shop, the van was already driving away.

Dan and Alex were standing looking in a shop window across the street.

'You'll never guess what!' said Matt to them.

'Rover!' shouted Alex and Dan at the same time.

'How did you know?' asked Hannah.

'We saw him come out and get into the van. He wasn't wearing his security guard uniform, but it was definitely Rover,' said Dan.

'Wow!' said Hannah. 'Alex, did you –'

'Yes, I took some photos,' replied Alex. She showed them the photos on her camera. The security guard was walking out of the shop, looking around, getting into the van.

'Good,' said Hannah. 'Maybe these will help us prove we were telling the truth.'

'What do they prove?' said Alex. 'They're just pictures of a man and a van.'

'Well ... why was Rover here? What's he doing in that van?' said Hannah.

'He's working with the robbers, that's what he's doing!' replied Matt. 'Think about it. He works at Mayfield House, and there was a robbery there. We found those boxes in the farmhouse, and then you girls told the police. I think Rover saw you talking to them on Wednesday – or maybe he found out from Miss Holt. And after that, the boxes disappeared.'

'You think Rover told the others?' said Dan.

'Yes,' said Matt. 'He told them the police were going to the house, and to go back and get the boxes out of there.'

'Maybe they took the boxes away after we left the house on Tuesday?' said Hannah.

'No, they were only going to take three boxes that day,' said Matt. 'We heard them say that, didn't we, Alex?'

Alex nodded.

'But all those boxes!' said Dan. 'How many were there? Twenty? Thirty? Their van isn't big enough to take them all in one trip.'

'Well, we don't know how much time they had,' said Matt.

'There's only one way to find out,' said Hannah.

'Can we speak to Officer Bryant or Officer Howes, please?' Hannah asked the police officer. Hannah and Alex were at the front desk of the town's police station.

'Yes, just a minute,' said the officer, and went into another room.

Officer Howes came out and said, 'Oh, hello. We spoke yesterday, didn't we? Is everything okay? How can I help you?'

'Well, we've been thinking about what we told you,' said Hannah. 'We just wanted to know one thing. After we spoke to you, how long was it before you went to the farmhouse?'

Officer Howes looked at the girls for a moment and then said, 'Girls, it was good that you spoke to us, but it really is best to leave police work to the police. I don't know what you think you saw. But I can tell you there was nothing at that house yesterday. Officer Bryant and I searched the place thoroughly.'

Hannah smiled and said, 'Of course, I understand. But we just wanted to know when you went.'

Officer Howes smiled back and said, 'Well, we had a few other things to do first. I think it was about an hour and a half after we spoke to you. Now I do need to remind you of what we said yesterday. Please stay away from the farmhouse. It's probably best that you enjoy your stay at the house and just worry about your schoolwork.'

'Yes sir, thank you for your help,' Hannah said sweetly. The girls left the police station quickly and found the boys sitting on a park bench nearby.

'Okay, guys, let's think,' said Matt. They had found a café and were sitting with a milkshake each. 'The robbers knew the police were coming. But they didn't know how much time they had. Their van isn't big enough to carry all the boxes in one trip.'

'There's only one road into the farm – the police had to come down that road,' said Hannah. 'So they had to move very quickly. If they filled the van with half of the boxes ...'

'... Where did they put the other half?' said Matt. 'They have to still be there somewhere.'

'But the police searched the place and found nothing,' said Alex.

'We need to go back to the farmhouse. Maybe the police missed something,' said Matt.

'Good idea,' said Hannah. 'We need to prove that we saw the boxes there.'

'But why do we want to prove anything?' asked Alex. 'Remember, we're supposed to be helping Dan stay out of trouble. Not getting him into more trouble.'

Dan looked at Alex. 'Actually, I've been thinking. I want to prove it, Alex. I want to show people that I am not just a silly school boy who gets into trouble.'

'We don't think that,' said Alex.

'No, but they do – the teachers and those police officers think that. I want to show them. I want to show my mum too. Please, Alex,' said Dan.

They all looked at Alex.

'Well, okay,' said Alex. 'But let's talk about it tonight. We need to meet the teachers and all the others in half an hour.'

That evening, Matt and Hannah found a quiet corner in the dining room to have a chat.

'So what is this great idea of yours?' asked Hannah.

'I think it's more of a crazy idea,' laughed Matt. He took a deep breath. 'I was thinking we need to find a way to embarrass Ethan. Then Dan can use that to stand up to him. Bullies always leave you alone if you stand up to them.'

'Okay, but how do we embarrass Ethan?' asked Hannah.

'Do you remember when Sarah showed us the paintings of Lord and Lady Langford? Simon said Ethan looked like Lord Langford.' Hannah nodded. 'Well I was thinking, maybe Lady Mary could pay Ethan a little visit in the night.'

Hannah clapped her hands in delight. 'Yes!' she cried. 'But how are you going to get a ghost to visit him in his room?'

Matt put his hand in his pocket and pulled out a long black and white feather.

'Meet Lady Mary!' he lightly brushed the feather against Hannah's cheek and neck.

Hannah shuddered and pushed the feather away.

'Hannah, it's not real. There is no Lady Mary ghost, you know.'

Hannah shuddered again. 'You don't know that for sure. That thing is creepy. I still don't see how you are going to do it.'

'Okay, here's my plan ...' began Matt. He quietly explained his plan to Hannah. The thought of Ethan being scared by a ghost made them giggle. They didn't notice Alex come up to the table.

'What are you two giggling about?' she asked as she sat down.

'Oh, nothing,' said Hannah innocently. 'We were just waiting for you two.'

'Dan's getting us hot chocolates. I hope you have got a good plan for how we get back to the farmhouse?'

'Oh, yes,' giggled Hannah. 'We've got lots of great plans!'

Chapter 5 The secret

Alex and Hannah carried their breakfast trays over to the table. They sat down next to Dan and Matt.

'Good morning,' said Hannah. 'How was your night?' She looked at Matt and he gave her a slight nod.

'Quite lively, actually,' said Dan.

'Lively? Why?' asked Alex.

'I was woken up by shouting next door,' replied Dan. 'Apparently Ethan had a nightmare. He was in a bit of a state about it!'

'Really?' asked Hannah, without looking at Matt.

'Yes,' Dan carried on. 'He woke up screaming, shouting something about ghosts. Tom said when they turned on the light he was hitting his cheek and shouting 'Go away! Leave me alone! They think he might have been crying'.

Hannah started to laugh and nearly choked on her juice.

'Oh, don't laugh,' said Alex. 'I feel a bit sorry for him. Look at him! He looks like he hasn't slept at all.'

The friends looked over at Ethan. Alex was right. He had dark circles under his eyes and he wasn't talking to anyone.

'He's certainly quieter than usual,' said Dan.

'Well, I don't feel sorry for him,' said Hannah. 'Maybe he'll be too tired to annoy us today!'

'Are we ready for today?' asked Matt. 'We're all agreed? We're going to check out the farmhouse again?'

The others nodded. They cleared their breakfast trays away and headed outside. Some of the students were already waiting for the teachers.

'All right, everyone,' called Mr Jones. 'Pay attention, please. It's hard to believe that it is our last day already. As you know we leave straight after breakfast tomorrow. But today we get to have some fun. We are going to start with a scavenger hunt.

Then this afternoon you can have some free time to pack and tidy up. Tonight we have a special dinner and 'disco'. If you are really good, I'll entertain you with some of my famous dance moves.'

The students groaned good-naturedly. Everyone liked Mr Jones.

'I've got your lists for the scavenger hunt here,' he continued. He came down the steps and walked around the students. He handed each group a plastic bag with a list inside. When he reached Ethan's group, he stopped and looked at Ethan carefully.

'Are you okay, Ethan?' he asked. 'You look very tired.'

'Yeah, I'm okay,' muttered Ethan, grumpily.

'Mm, maybe no cheese for you tonight at dinner, hey boy?' said Mr Jones cheerfully.

Matt put his hand over his mouth quickly, to stop himself laughing.

'What's he talking about?' whispered Alex.

'They say eating cheese late at night gives you nightmares,' giggled Matt. 'Mr Jones must have heard about Ethan's nightmare last night.'

'Now, if you all look at your lists, you'll see there are twenty things for you to find,' said Mr Jones. 'Your job is to find one of each thing in the gardens and grounds of Mayfield House. Gardens and grounds only, everyone. No one should be in the lodge or the house. The first group to come back with all twenty things will be the winners of the scavenger hunt. I want everyone to be back here within three hours, please. And remember – have fun! Let's begin.'

'Okay, what's on the list?' asked Hannah.

'But we're going to the farmhouse, aren't we?' said Matt.

'I know, but we have to do some of the hunt,' said Hannah. 'If we don't do any of it, the teachers will know something is wrong.'

'Okay,' said Alex. She had the list. 'A black feather, a white stone, a pink flower –'

'Oh, this is for babies,' said Dan.

'Well, let's do ten minutes of it. Then when everyone is busy we can get away to the farm,' said Hannah.

'I can help with number one,' said Matt as he pulled a feather from his backpack. 'It's black and white. Do you think that's ok?'

'Sure,' said Alex, taking the feather and putting it in the plastic bag with the list. 'But why have you got a feather in your bag?'

'No reason,' said Matt, trying not to look at Hannah. 'I just thought it looked nice and might be useful for my project.'

Matt smiled to himself as he followed his friends. He had enjoyed playing the ghost last night.

They found a multi-coloured leaf and a white stone as they walked to where there was a gate behind some trees. They slipped through the gate and hurried down a path away from the grounds of the house. As they got to the road and walked around a bend, Hannah groaned.

'What are they doing here?' she said.

Ahead of them were Ethan and Chris. Before they had a chance to hide, the two boys turned and saw them.

'Well, look who's out of school grounds,' said Ethan. 'Poor little Dan had better not get caught.'

'Shut up Ethan,' said Dan. 'Anyway, why are you out of school grounds?'

'We're not doing a stupid scavenger hunt,' said Ethan.

'Maybe you should go on a ghost hunt instead,' said Hannah. Before Ethan had a chance to answer they walked off up the road. Once out of sight, they climbed over a gate and headed across a field to join the footpath that led to the farmhouse.

It was a much nicer walk on a sunny day. Forty minutes later they walked through the front door of the farmhouse. They checked all the rooms, but they were empty.

'The police were right,' said Alex. 'The boxes have gone.'

'Maybe there's an attic in the roof,' said Hannah, looking up at the ceiling.

'That would have taken too long, they'd need a ladder,' said Matt. 'It would take ages to put them up there one by one.'

'Let's have a look outside,' said Dan.

'Wait,' said Alex, looking worried. 'If the boxes are here somewhere, then maybe the robbers will come back. We need to be careful.'

'Well, we have to look, now that we're here,' said Matt. 'Let's go to the barn.'

They walked over to the barn.

'It's just like it was before when we were in here,' said Hannah. 'There's just this old tractor.'

'No, wait. Look at this,' said Matt. He pointed at the floor in the corner. 'There are footprints all around here.'

'You're right,' said Hannah. 'I don't remember seeing these old sacks either.'

There was a pile of empty old sacks near the footprints.

Dan bent down and moved them. 'There's a trapdoor in the floor here,' he said.

'Can you open it?' asked Alex.

'Yes, I think so,' said Dan. He bent down and pulled the trap-door open. 'It's a cellar. It's really dark. I can't see anything in there.'

'Here, you can use the torch on my phone,' said Hannah.

She handed her phone to Dan and he shone it down into the open trap door.

'There's a ladder here,' said Dan. 'I'm going to climb down.'

'Be careful,' said Alex. They waited as Dan climbed down the ladder.

'Hey!' he called to them. 'The boxes are down here.'

'Are you sure they are the same boxes?' asked Hannah.

'I think so,' said Dan. They all waited. 'It's not all of them, but ... yes, yes, here are some of the things we saw.'

'Well done, Dan,' said Hannah.

'Okay, what do we do now?' asked Matt.

'We call the police,' said Hannah.

'And what do we tell them? We've found the boxes? They won't believe us,' said Matt.

'Here,' said Alex, holding out her camera. 'My camera's got a good flash. Take some photos of the boxes.'

She handed the camera down to Dan.

A few minutes later he climbed out. 'I got some photos,' he said. 'I'll take a couple of the trap door and the barn too. Then I think we should get out of here.'

'Yes,' said Hannah. 'We need to get back before the others finish the scavenger hunt, anyway.'

Matt and Alex led the way back to the footpath behind the barn.

'What do we do now?' asked Alex.

'With those photos, it's time to go to the police,' said Hannah.

'Hey, I can hear a car or something,' said Matt.

They turned and looked back at the farm. The white van was driving down the road to the front of the farmhouse.

'They're back,' said Matt.

'I bet they've come to take the rest of the boxes away,' said Dan.

'Let's get some photos of the van. That will prove they were at the farm,' said Alex taking out her camera.

They walked back to the end of the footpath and hid behind a bush. Alex took some photos of the van.

'Can you get some pictures of the men?' said Matt.

'We are too far away to really get their faces,' said Alex.

'I want to go closer and get photos of their faces,' said Dan.

'No,' said Alex. 'They'll see you.'

'We'll stay hidden behind the barn,' said Dan. 'Are you coming, Matt?'

'Yeah,' replied Matt. 'You hold on to your camera, Alex. I can use my phone to take pictures.'

The boys ran down behind the farmhouse to the side of the barn.

'I don't like this,' said Alex to Hannah.

'No,' said Hannah. 'I hope they don't take too long.'

Matt and Dan hid outside the barn. Dan looked through a hole in the barn wall.

'What are they saying?' whispered Matt.

'I'm not sure,' said Dan. 'They're arguing, as usual ... something about where to put the boxes now. They're talking about the police coming back.'

'Can you get a photo?' said Matt. He held out his mobile phone.

'No, wait until they come out,' said Dan.

From where the girls were hiding, they couldn't see the boys. But they did see a car drive down the road and park behind the van.

'Oh, no. Who's this?' said Alex.

'I don't know,' said Hannah. 'Wait. Someone's getting out of the car. It's Rover!'

'Are you sure?' asked Alex.

'Yes,' said Hannah. 'We have to tell the boys.'

'But we can't run down to them. He'll see us,' said Alex.

'I'll send them a text,' said Hannah. 'Quick, Alex, get a photo of Rover before he moves away.'

Hannah quickly sent a text to Matt's mobile phone: *Rover here – hide*!

'I hope they're okay,' said Hannah. 'I'm going to wait until Rover goes around the back of the farmhouse. Then I'll go down a bit closer, so I can see. You stay here.'

'Okay, but be careful,' said Alex.

'I wish they'd stop arguing and bring some boxes out,' said Dan.

'I want to get the photos and get out of here,' said Matt. The phone in his hands vibrated. 'Wait, I've got a message.'

At the same time, he felt a hand on his shoulder. It was Rover.

'What do we have here then?' said Rover. 'Come on get up.'

He dragged Matt and Dan to their feet.

Hannah saw Rover take the boys into the barn. She ran back to Alex.

'Alex, he got them!' she said. 'Rover caught Dan and Matt. He took them into the barn!'

'Oh, no!' cried Alex. 'We need help. Phone Mrs Turner.'

Hannah reached for her phone and called Mrs Turner.

'She's not answering,' she said.

'We don't have time for this,' said Alex. 'We have to get help.'

'Let's go back up the footpath. We can't let them see us,' said Hannah. 'Come on!'

The girls ran as fast as they could.

Rover pushed Dan and Matt to the floor roughly. The boys looked at each other. They were very scared.

The boxes were out of the cellar now. They were piled up on the floor near the trapdoor.

Rover and the three men looked at the boys.

'Who are they?' asked one of the men.

'I don't know,' said Rover. 'I found them outside. They were watching you.'

'Look in their pockets,' said another of the men. 'Take their phones off them. Are they alone?'

'I didn't see anyone else out there,' said Rover.

One of the men came up close to the boys. 'What are you doing here?' he asked. 'What do you want?'

'Nothing,' said Dan. 'We heard some kids talking about the old farmhouse. We just wanted to look around.'

'What kids?' he said.

'That's where I've seen them before,' said Rover. 'They're part of the school group up at the house.'

'Why were you hiding out there?' asked the man.

'We heard voices. We just wanted to see what was going on,' said Dan.

'What did you hear?' asked Rover.

'Not much,' answered Dan. 'We weren't there long. We heard you arguing.'

'They're just a couple of nosey kids. Come on, we're wasting time. I want to get out of here.'

'So do I, but what are we going to do with them now?' asked the first man.

'Let's tie them up. Make sure they don't run off,' said Rover. 'I don't want them telling anyone about us.'

The men tied the boys' hands behind their backs with rope. They tied their ankles together, and then they tied them to the front of the old tractor. The boys couldn't move.

'Let's get the boxes in the van,' said the second man. 'Come on. This is the last lot of boxes. We don't need to come back after this.'

'Shall we take these kids with us?' said the third man.

'And do what with them? The school will call the police when they find they're missing. Then the police will be everywhere looking for them,' said the first man.

'I don't want to touch them' said the third man. 'We agreed – nobody gets hurt, remember?'

'I say we leave them here,' said the second man. 'Let's get the boxes out of here and go. By the time they find them, we'll be far away.'

'No,' said Rover. 'This is the first place the police will look. We can't take the risk. We have to take them with us.'

'And then what?' shouted one of the men. 'I would never have signed up for this if I thought we were going to be hurting kids.'

'We're not going to hurt them,' said Rover. 'I just want to buy us some time. We need to make sure we have plenty of

time to get away. Stick them in the van and we can drop them off when we get clear of here. By the time they walk home and raise the alarm, we'll be long gone. Put some of those boxes in my car. Make sure there's room for these two in the van.'

The four men carried the boxes outside. When they had finished, Rover came back to the boys. He untied them from the front of the tractor and then untied their feet. He pulled them up roughly. Then he re-tied their hands tightly behind their backs. He pushed them out of the barn and round to the front of the house. The back doors of the van were open. He pushed the boys into the van.

'Now, you sit there nice and quietly,' he said. 'We're going for fun little ride.'

Chapter 6 The whole story

Hannah and Alex ran through the gates of Mayfield House. Some of the students were still finishing the scavenger hunt.

'Where's Mrs Turner?' gasped Hannah, barely able to breathe.

'She was here a minute ago,' said one of the girls. 'I think she went to the lodge. You guys are in so much trouble!'

'What do you mean?' asked Alex. 'What trouble?'

'The teachers know you left the grounds. They've been looking for you,' answered the girl.

'How ...?' Alex started to say.

'Ethan!' said Hannah. 'That's how!'

Alex looked at Hannah in horror. Hannah grabbed her arm.

'Come on! We don't have time to waste!' she reminded her.

The girls ran to the lodge. Mrs Turner was in the study room. They didn't wait to knock but ran straight in the room.

'Hannah! Alex!' cried Mrs Turner, standing up. 'Where on earth have you been? Where are the boys? Do you know how much trouble you've caused?'

'Mrs Turner, you have to help them! The man took them into the barn. You have to call the police. We have to save them!' cried Hannah.

'What are you talking about?' said Mrs Turner. 'Look at the two of you. Have you been running? Who do we have to save? Come and sit down. Now take a breath and let's start again.'

'Please, we don't have time!' said Hannah.

'Hannah, you need to calm down,' said Mrs Turner, 'I don't understand a word you're saying. You need to explain to me why you left the grounds and where the boys are.'

'I'm trying to tell you where the boys are!' shouted Hannah, getting annoyed.

'Mrs Turner, I can explain,' said Alex more calmly. She realised they weren't getting anywhere by panicking. She sat down and told Mrs Turner the whole story. Then she took out her camera. She showed her the photos that proved she was telling the truth.

Mrs Turner listened carefully and looked at the photos. When they had finished, she reached for her phone. The girls listened as she talked to the police. Finally she put the phone down and looked at Hannah and Alex.

'The police are heading to the farm as we speak. Try not to panic, girls. I'm sure the boys will be okay,' she smiled reassuringly at them. 'You do understand that we will have to talk about the fact that you left the school grounds as well. But for now the police have asked us to go down to the station. They will need to take statements from both of you. They also want copies of all your photos, Alex.'

'Mrs Turner, did Ethan tell you that we had left the grounds?' asked Hannah.

Mrs Turner paused for a moment, she seemed to be trying to decide something. Finally she spoke.

'I'm not sure I should tell you this, but yes Ethan told me,' she said. 'He said he saw you leave the grounds through the back gate and walk down the path to the road.'

'But that's a lie!' exclaimed Hannah.

'I'm sorry, what's a lie?' asked Mrs Turner. 'I don't think you can pretend you didn't leave do you?'

'No, of course not,' said Hannah, she looked at Alex questioningly. Alex nodded. Hannah took a deep breath and continued. 'It's a lie that Ethan saw us leave. We met Ethan up the road. He was out of school grounds too!'

'Oh, was he now!' said Mrs Turner. 'Come on, we'd better get to the station. Maybe in the car you two girls can explain what is going on between you four and Ethan.'

Dan and Matt were sitting in the back of the van, squashed in with the boxes. The van was travelling fast down the winding country roads. It was hard for them to stay upright with their hands tied together.

'Do you think they're just going to dump us somewhere?' Dan asked Matt.

'Yes,' said Matt reassuringly. 'At least, I hope so. You heard what they said. They don't want to hurt anyone. I wish we could see where we are going.'

Dan twisted around and tried to get a look at the men in the front seat, but there were too many boxes in the way.

'It's no good. I can't see anything,' he said.

Matt tried to get on his knees to look out over the top of the boxes. But he lost his balance and fell on Dan.

'Ouch, watch it,' said Dan.

'It's no good, I can't stay upright. I don't think we're on the country roads anymore, though. I can hear lots of cars, I think we're on a main road now.'

'Can you get your hands free?' Dan asked.

'No, the knots are too tight,' said Matt.

'Same here,' said Dan.

'I wonder what happened to the girls?' said Dan. 'Do you think they got back to the house okay?'

'I hope so. I hope they managed to get some help,' said Matt. 'Hey can you hear that?'

Above the sound of the engine the boys heard the sound of sirens in the distance

'Police!' cried Dan. 'I hope they are coming for us!'

The three men started arguing. The boys felt the van speed up and start to weave in and out of the traffic.

'Oh, no! They're going to try and get away,' said Dan.

'I wish we could get these ties undone,' said Matt, wriggling his hands to get free. 'I hope we don't crash!'

The sirens were close now. The boys heard them pass the van and grow fainter as the police cars sped further up the road.

'Where are they going?' cried Dan. 'Do you think they've missed us?'

But just then they heard more sirens approaching. This time they came right up behind the van.

'Pull over!'

The men started shouting at each other again. But finally the boys felt the van slowing, pulling over and stopping at the side of the road. The boys heard car doors slamming and shouting as the police surrounded the van. They pulled the men from the front of the van and quickly handcuffed them.

A minute later, the back door of the van opened. Police Officer Bryant looked at them.

'Are you boys okay?' he asked. He helped them out of the van and untied their hands.

The boys looked around them. There seemed to be police cars everywhere. The three men were sitting on the grass verge. Their hands were handcuffed behind them. The police were searching the back of the van.

Officer Bryant helped the boys into the back of a nearby police car.

'I'll take you back to the police station in town,' he said. 'Mrs Turner and your friends are already there. We need to have a little chat!'

As Officer Bryant drove them up the road the boys could see more police cars up ahead. As they drove past they saw Rover in handcuffs, being put into a police car.

'Now, he's a charming man!' said Officer Bryant sarcastically. 'He tried to get away and leave the others to take the blame.'

An hour later, the boys were sitting in a room at the police station. Hannah, Alex and Mrs Turner were with them. Officer Bryant and Officer Howes were there too.

Officer Bryant looked at the notes he had written down. Alex's photos had been printed out. The prints were laid out in front of him.

'We are sure that we can prove these men are the robbers. These photos are a great help. They are very clear. You're a good photographer, young lady,' he said to Alex.

'Thank you,' replied Alex, smiling.

'We have been working on this case for three months. Mayfield House wasn't the only place they had robbed,' said Officer Howes. 'It will be good to send these four men to jail. Four less criminals on our streets.'

'It's been quite an interesting school trip for you four,' said Officer Bryant. 'Perhaps a bit more interesting than your teachers planned?'

'They certainly had an unusual scavenger hunt!' said Mrs Turner with a smile, 'I don't remember seeing criminals on the list of things to collect!'

'Well, I think we have everything we need for today,' said Officer Bryant, 'I'm sure you all want to get back to the house.'

'There's a reward for what you four did,' added Officer Howes. 'Did you know that?'

Hannah, Alex, Dan and Matt looked at each other in surprise. Hannah was the first to speak, 'No, sir. We didn't know there was a reward.'

'Oh, yes there's often a reward for things like this,' said Officer Howes. 'It's for people who help us to solve cases. Especially tough cases like this. We have wanted to catch George Roberts for a long time. He's a very nasty man.'

'We don't advise members of the public to get involved with criminals. Especially when they are as young as you four. But you have been a huge help,' said Officer Bryant. 'You're very lucky that you weren't hurt, though. I hope you will never get so involved again!'

'No sir,' they replied together.

'One of our officers will drive you back now. But we will need to talk to you again.'

'Yes, of course,' said Mrs Turner. 'You have all our phone numbers.'

They arrived back at the lodge in two police cars. As they got out of the cars, all the students surrounded them. They all wanted to talk to them and hear about their great adventure.

'Now, everyone, that's enough,' shouted Mrs Turner. 'Give these four some air to breathe. We need to go inside now.'

She turned to the four friends and said, 'The first thing you need to do is to phone your parents. They were very worried about you. Mr Jones has spoken to them all and told them you are all safe. They are waiting to hear from you.'

As they walked past the other students, Ethan and Chris pushed into Dan.

'Hey, hero,' said Ethan nastily. 'A robber catches a robber! Funny, hey? I don't think you're a hero at all.'

Dan turned to Ethan and smiled nicely. 'I'm not trying to be a hero, Ethan, and neither were you last night, from what I hear.' He pulled some tissues out of his pocket and threw them at Ethan. 'Here, just in case your little ghost comes back tonight.'

Ethan's face turned red, but he was silent. Dan walked past him, his head held high and a big smile on his face. Hannah and Matt smiled at each other. Somehow they knew that Ethan wouldn't be bothering Dan ever again. As Alex and Dan walked into the lodge, Mrs Turner turned to Matt and Hannah.

'It is funny how that ghost chose to visit Ethan, isn't it?' she said, watching them carefully.

Matt and Hannah looked shocked but said nothing. Mrs Turner laughed. She put her finger to her lips and winked at them. Then she walked ahead into the lodge.

The next morning at breakfast, Mrs Turner stood up. She waited for the students to be quiet.

'As you know, we had an unusual day yesterday. We are due to leave this morning. But we have been asked to leave one hour later. We have some reporters from the local papers coming to talk to our heroes,' she said. 'Hannah, Alex, Dan and Matt, can you come with me, please?'

They found Officer Bryant waiting for them in the study room. He talked to them about the questions the reporters were going to ask. He wished them luck and left.

Mrs Turner closed the door behind him and turned to look at them.

'I spoke to our head teacher last night. He asked me to congratulate you on helping to catch the robbers yesterday. He also said he wants to see you in his office first thing on Monday morning.'

'He's not going to expel Dan is he?' cried Hannah. 'That's so unfair. It wasn't just Dan, we all –'

'No, Hannah,' Mrs Turner interrupted. 'Dan is not going to be expelled from school. But you have broken quite a few school rules. I'm sure Mr Ross has a useful punishment planned for you four, and for Ethan and Chris. I may have heard him mention something about gardening.'

The four friends groaned.

'Now, come on. We don't want to keep your fans waiting. Do we?'

They followed Mrs Turner outside. A group of reporters was waiting to talk to them. They were surprised to see a TV camera there too.

'Nobody said anything about TV!' Alex whispered to Hannah.

'I know! I'm a bit nervous,' replied Hannah.

The reporters started to ask them some questions.

One of the reporters put a microphone in front of Dan. 'How does it feel to be a hero?' she asked.

Dan opened his mouth to answer, but nothing came out. Hannah stepped in front of him. 'We don't think we are heroes,' she said.

'What are you going to do with the reward money?' asked another reporter.

Hannah looked at Alex and Matt. They smiled and nodded. 'I think Dan can answer that question,' she said, and moved back.

The reporter held the microphone in front of Dan again. 'Well?' she demanded.

Dan lifted his head and looked at his friends. He stepped forward and looked at the reporter. 'I'd like to say something first. I have been in a bit of trouble this year. I did some silly things, but I've changed. I've learnt my lesson. I want to say sorry to my mum ... and to my dad. I've put them through a lot and made them worry about me. But most of all I want to say thanks to my friends Hannah, Alex and Matt. They have been there for me every day. We've decided that we want to give the reward money to charity. We are going to give it to a charity that helps young people who are in trouble.'

The students started clapping and cheering. Hannah, Alex and Matt stood beside Dan. The four friends smiled as the reporters took photos.

'I hope they take a good photo,' said Alex to her friends. They all laughed.